W9-DES-527

The Wedding

by Angela Johnson

pictures by David Soman

ORCHARD BOOKS NEW YORK

Orchard Books, A Grolier Company, 95 Madison Avenue, New York, NY 10016

Manufactured in the United States of America. Printed and bound by Phoenix Color Corp. Book design by Mina Greenstein.
The text of this book is set in 16 point Esprit Medium. The illustrations are collage. 10 9 8 7 6 5 4 3 2 1

Library of Congress Cataloging-in-Publication Data
Johnson, Angela. The wedding / by Angela Johnson ; illustrated by David Soman. p. cm.
Summary: Daisy describes the preparations leading up to her older sister's wedding and the joyous and bittersweet feelings surrounding the event itself.
ISBN 0-531-30139-7 (trade : alk. paper).—ISBN 0-531-33139-3 (lib. bdg. : alk. paper)
[1. Weddings—Fiction. 2. Sisters—Fiction. 3. Afro-Americans—Fiction.] I. Soman, David, ill. II. Title.
PZ7.J629We 1999 [E]—dc21 98-36163

To Norma Zimmerman,
with much love

—A.J.

For Ellen and Doug

—D.S.

*S*ister and Jamal told us about the wedding the first day of spring.

Now that the leaves are falling,
there is the wedding.

Long dresses,
flowers,
wrapped boxes,

and tissue-paper rooms—
with everybody saying
“Congratulations,”

and me,
Daisy,
all around the room,
thinking about being
in the wedding. . . .

Sister with Mama and me,
trying on her dress,

tasting food,

and looking at rooms
to have the wedding
when the leaves start to fall. . . .

Me thinking about the wedding
and Sister leaving me
and us
and here
after the wedding.

And I will walk by everybody
carrying flowers and smiling—

being in the wedding.

They will cry when they see
Sister.
Me too. . . .

Then the food, music, and
dancing will make them
smile again.

I will dance with Jamal there,
who will take Sister from me
and us

and here—
but leave them together.

And Mama and Daddy will cry,
and Uncle Joe will squeeze everyone,

and all the relatives and friends will eat till
their plates are empty
and the moon is shining on the trees.

Then, when it is all over
and the tissue-paper rooms are
quiet
and the flowers are gone
but the leaves are still falling,
I will be there—

thinking about it all,
thinking about the wedding.